TERRAN

THE
CHINESE GHOST
INCIDENT

Piccadilly Press • London

Terrance Dicks lives in North London. He has written many books
for Piccadilly Press including the CHANGING UNIVERSE series
and the SECOND SIGHT series.

Also available in this series: *The Bermuda Triangle Incident,
The Borley Rectory Incident, The Circle of Death Incident, The Easter
Island Incident, The Inca Alien Incident, The Mafia Incident, The Nazi
Dagger Incident, The Pyramid Incident, The Transylvanian Incident*
and *The Wollagong Incident.*

PROLOGUE

The night wind whistled eerily through the vast deserted building site. Tarpaulins flapped in sudden gusts, piles of stone, lumber and steel scaffolding creaked and groaned uneasily.

Black clouds scudded across the moon so that the site was sometimes brightly lit, sometimes plunged into darkness.

Bracing himself against the night winds, Big Han, the chief night watchman, continued methodically on his rounds. Perhaps there was a hurricane on the way, he thought. This was the monsoon season, and typhoons were frequent in the South China Sea. Usually they missed Hong Kong – but even a near miss could cause high winds, heavy rains and flooding. This site was right down on the harbour.

Big Han shrugged, said a brief prayer to his ancestors and went on his way. He couldn't do anything about the weather, but he could see to it that his team of night-watchmen did their jobs properly. On nights like this the lazy devils tried to grab a quiet cigarette, or even a nap, in some hidden corner.

That wouldn't do at all. Hong Kong was an active, enterprising place, and its thieves were even more enterprising than its businessmen. There was a lot of valuable material on the site. Thanks to all the delays it had been standing there for far too long. It wouldn't do to get careless – or by the time things got going again, half the material would have melted mysteriously away.

Big Han had already been offered a handsome bribe to turn a blind eye to a bit of thieving. Some young squirt from the Triad had approached him in his local bar. Big Han had flattened him with a casual swipe. The squirt had picked himself up and scuttled away, breathing bloodthirsty threats of Triad vengeance.

Big Han smiled at the memory. He wasn't frightened of the Triads – or of anything else, come to that. Except, perhaps, of ghosts. Every sensible man feared the spirits. Now, as if they didn't have enough troubles, there were all these rumours that the site was haunted.

Big Han shivered. The project had certainly had more than its share of problems. If some angry malignant spirit, one whose descendants had neglected the proper prayers and sacrifices, was roaming the site, it would explain much . . .

Suddenly he saw a glow somewhere in the distance. A light where no light should be. Thieves! And nobody had given the alarm. Grasping his heavy staff, Big Han hurried forwards.

He rounded a big stack of lumber and paused in horror.

One of his watchmen lay on the ground in a pool of blood.

Hovering above the man was a glowing shape, a tall, thin, ghostly figure in flowing robes. It had long moustaches, burning red eyes, and a face twisted in diabolical rage . . .

Big Han stood, transfixed in horror.

The glowing shape raised a threatening hand.

Big Han felt an invisible force hurl him backwards as the stack of lumber began toppling towards the ground.

The glowing shape hovered for a moment longer and then faded away . . .

Chapter One

JOURNEY INTO DANGER

It was night and I was standing on a rocky hillside, overlooking a steep-roofed pagoda. Beyond the pagoda was the sea. Two arms of coastline curved round to enclose a tranquil moonlit bay. Across the bay glided a triangular-sailed junk.

Suddenly a tall, white-robed figure swooped towards me through the darkness. Its long, thin face was twisted in anger and its eyes burned red.

I had a sudden feeling of dread, of desperate danger.

And there was something else.

The angry ghost was trying to tell me something . . .

Something vitally important.

Somehow the message just wasn't getting through.

Angrily, the figure reached out a claw-like hand. As if determined to make me pay attention, it grabbed my shoulder with long bony fingers, shaking me hard.

It had a surprisingly strong grip for a ghost . . .

* * *

'Wake up, Matthew, wake up!'

I opened my eyes, and the Chinese ghost turned into Dad, vigorously shaking my shoulder.

He looked down at me with concern. 'Are you all right? You were muttering and moaning . . .'

I blinked, trying to remember where I was.

I was sitting in a high-backed seat next to an oval window with a view of clouds. Dad sat next to me in a similar seat.

There was a low hum of engine noise . . .

I was on a plane, and we were going to Hong Kong – to hunt for a Chinese ghost.

Only it looked as if the ghost was hunting for us.

I yawned and rubbed my eyes. 'Sorry . . . I don't usually sleep on planes.'

'On a thirteen-hour flight, a little nap is very understandable,' said Dad drily. 'Were you having a nightmare?'

'I suppose so . . .'

'What about?'

'I'm not sure. Some kind of Chinese ghost . . .'

'Very appropriate!' said Dad.

I'm Matt Stirling, and Dad's Professor James Stirling. Dad used to be a big wheel in the space race, but these days things are very different. He's

7

now head of the Paranormal Studies department of an American scientific research institute.

As a matter of fact he pretty well *is* the Paranormal Studies department. I'm his assistant.

As it happened, we'd got to know each other again not that long ago, not just as working colleagues but as father and son.

Mum and Dad had split up when I was still a baby. When Mum got killed in an accident I was brought up by relatives, and when they retired to live abroad I was passed on to Dad.

Suddenly he found himself landed with a teenage son he hadn't seen for years – just when he was out of a job.

As I said, Dad's a top space scientist – or he was, until the funding for his space research suddenly dried up. Fortunately, the Paranormal Studies job popped up at the same time as I did. Dad took the job, took over my education, and took me on as his assistant.

Professionally, things worked out pretty well.

Dad's a sceptic about the paranormal, while I like to keep an open mind. It isn't a bad combination.

On the family front, things are a bit trickier.

Dad's used to being a big cheese in the scientific community. He's also used to instant obedience, universal admiration and complete agreement with anything he says.

None of which he gets from me.

All in all we don't get along too badly. In fact, I think I can say I'm gradually civilising him, though it's a long hard job.

So, here we were on our way to Hong Kong.

We were making the trip at the request of Ms Alexander, a very formidable lady indeed. She wore high-powered business suits and serious glasses, and looked like the first woman president of some big City corporation. She was, in fact, director of a top-secret security department – one that takes over whenever something particularly weird is worrying the intelligence community.

When that happened, Ms Alexander sometimes called on us for help. She'd summoned us to her Thames-side office for a conference about this Chinese ghost business.

At first, Dad hadn't been too keen on going to Hong Kong. 'I've already been to Hong Kong,' he said peevishly. 'I attended several scientific con-ferences there – in the days when I was a proper scientist, instead of a spook hunter.'

Ms Alexander smiled. 'Well, it's in your role as a spook hunter that I need your help.'

Dad had gone on grumbling. 'Anyway, Hong Kong's no longer our responsibility. We handed it back to China a few years ago.'

Ms Alexander nodded. 'That's right, in nineteen ninety-seven. But, in a way, that only makes Hong Kong even more important.'

'Why?'

'It's important for world peace to bring China into the twenty-first century, to strengthen links with the West. Hong Kong is a sort of bridge,' said Ms Alexander. She smiled. 'Some people fear that Hong Kong will end up like the rest of China. But some of us hope China will end up like Hong Kong!'

'And what has all this got to do with us?' asked Dad.

'The British and Chinese governments are co-operating on a number of projects. One of the biggest is the redevelopment of a big site near the harbour. A British-based construction outfit is carrying out the work.' She paused. 'They've run into a lot of trouble.'

'What sort of trouble?' I asked.

'You name it. Financial trouble, labour trouble, accidents, possibly sabotage . . .' She paused again, as if wondering quite how to go on.

'There's something else, isn't there?' I said. 'Something – unusual. Otherwise you wouldn't have called us in.'

She nodded. 'I'm afraid so. For some time there have been persistent rumours that the site is haunted. Now there's been some sort of incident. Somebody's been killed and I gather the men are refusing to go back to work.'

'I see,' said Dad. 'Do we know who's been killed – and why? What happened exactly?'

'Did the ghost do it?' I asked.

'I've only had a brief preliminary report,' said Ms Alexander. 'Mr Wu will brief you fully when you arrive in Hong Kong. He is my opposite number in the Chinese Security Service . . .'

So now we were on our way to Hong Kong. In fact, after thirteen hours of flying, we were almost there. Dad looked at his watch. 'We'll be landing soon.'

A few minutes later the landing announcement came over the plane's public address system. All around me people began fastening their seat belts.

'Landing at Hong Kong airport was a real roller-coaster ride in the old days,' said Dad. 'Kaitak was right in the middle of Hong Kong.

Very tricky approach. Now we're landing at the new Chek Lap Kok airport. It's on Lantau Island, close to Hong Kong. I expect it will all be ultra-modern and boringly efficient.'

I yawned, rubbing my eyes. 'Fine by me,' I said. 'The last thing I want is exciting air travel. Anyway, I've been bored for the last thirteen hours, so why change now?'

Actually, it hadn't been too bad. When not dozing, I'd spent the flight brushing up on my studies of Hong Kong. I reckon the more you know about where you're going the better.

With the succession of meals, movies and drinks, followed by more meals, more movies and more drinks, the time had passed surprisingly quickly.

We made what seemed to be a smooth landing and the usual announcement about remaining quietly in our seats came over the intercom.

Our fellow passengers, a mixture of European and Chinese, ignored this completely, jumping to their feet, grabbing luggage from overhead lockers and jamming the aisles.

Dad stretched in his seat and yawned. 'I see Hong Kong hasn't changed!'

'How do you mean?'

'Hurry, hurry hurry, rush, rush rush! The first

man off the plane may be able to make a better business deal. Hong Kong is one of the most hard-working places in the world!'

When the aisles had cleared we collected our hand luggage and left the plane.

A medium-sized, slightly plump Chinese gentleman in horn-rimmed glasses and an immaculately tailored suit was waiting for us at the bottom of the exit ramp. Beside him stood a hatchet-faced character in army uniform.

The man in the suit stepped forward.

'Professor Stirling?'

Dad nodded. 'Mr Wu, I presume?'

The Chinese gentleman bowed. 'Precisely so,' he said in an impeccable upper-class English accent. 'Welcome to Hong Kong! This is my colleague from military intelligence, Major Chang.'

Major Chang clicked his heels and bowed. 'I am honoured to meet you.' His English, unlike Mr Wu's, was clipped and heavily accented.

'Ah, military intelligence!' said Dad. 'That's . . .'

He winced as I gave him a sharp kick on the ankle and concluded, '. . . that's very interesting.'

He'd been about to trot out his favourite old joke about military intelligence being a contradiction in terms. From the look of Major Chang I didn't think he'd appreciate it. Not many military men do.

Mr Wu bowed again. 'May I say what a great honour it is to meet you, Professor Stirling? I was privileged to attend several of your lectures during my time at Oxford.'

Dad did his best to look modest, never easy for him. 'You're very kind.'

Mr Wu turned to me. 'And this is, as we say in China, your number one son?'

'One and only, I'm afraid,' I said.

'You are fortunate in being blessed with such a distinguished father,' said Mr Wu. 'And you, professor, in being gifted with such a fine son. Now, shall we be on our way?'

He gestured towards an open-sided vehicle standing close by. It looked rather like those buggies you see on very expensive golf courses. A uniformed airport official sat at the wheel.

The buggy held two rows of backward-facing seats. Dad and I took one, and Mr Wu and Major Chang the other. The buggy set off towards the main airport building. Clearly we were far too important to have to walk.

Once we got there, I was glad of the buggy. The place was enormous. Mr Wu turned round. 'Twice the size of Heathrow,' he murmured proudly.

'I believe you!' I said.

We sped across the busy, crowded terminal at a surprising speed, lesser mortals leaping aside to get out of our way. We drove past an armed guard into a restricted area and stopped at an office. We produced our passports and diplomatic papers, Mr Wu snapped orders in Chinese and a respectful official bowed and stamped our papers.

Our luggage appeared from nowhere and a gang of porters loaded it on to the buggy.

Then it was back on the buggy for us as well, another trip through the vast terminal buildings and out on to a pillared arcade beside an access road where a long black limousine stood waiting.

Suddenly a tall, robed figure was rushing towards me, its long thin face scowling in fury. I had a feeling of terror – and an overwhelming sense of danger . . .

As the ghostly figure faded, I saw a jeep-like vehicle speeding down the road towards our buggy. It was filled with men – armed men.

'Look out!' I yelled.

The driver swung hard on the wheel and our buggy crashed into a pillar and tipped over, throwing us all clear.

Suddenly the air was filled with gunfire . . .

Chapter Two

DEATH IN HONG KONG

Things happened very fast after that.

Luckily the overturned buggy was between us and the terrorists, acting as a shield.

As bullets spanged into the overturned vehicle, I scrambled to my feet. I was dimly aware of Mr Wu and Major Chang jumping up as well.

Crouching low, I helped Dad up and dragged him behind the pillar – just as the jeep hit our buggy with a crash of screeching metal.

Mr Wu and Major Chang both had guns in their hands by now, and armed security guards were converging on the scene. The terrorists were soon caught in a deadly crossfire. There were four men in the jeep and three of them were shot down almost at once. Only one was left on his feet, a tall, gaunt Chinese with a bony skull-like face.

He stood, gazing desperately around him, some

kind of machine-pistol in his hand.

Mr Wu gestured towards the surrounding guards and shouted something, presumably ordering the man to surrender. The gaunt man hesitated, seemed about to obey. He raised the machine-pistol as if about to throw it down.

Major Chang fired twice, and the gaunt man staggered back and fell to the ground.

He went over to the gaunt man's body, and kicked the machine-pistol aside. 'Uzi,' he said. 'Or rather – cheap imitation of Uzi.'

He turned over the body with his foot so that it lay face down. He bent down and ripped open the tattered white shirt, revealing the man's back. It was entirely covered by an elaborate dragon-shaped tattoo.

'Triad!'

The Triad gangs, as I knew from my research, were China's equivalent of the Mafia.

'It is unfortunate that he could not be taken alive,' said Mr Wu stiffly. 'He might have given us valuable information about this attack.'

'They never talk,' said Major Chang dismissively. 'Besides, the gun was still in his hands. I dared not risk the lives of honoured guests.'

Mr Wu sighed. 'No doubt you are right. I must

leave matters here in your hands, Major Chang, while I see our guests to their hotel.' He turned to me and Dad. 'I am so sorry that this has happened. Are you both unharmed?'

Dad glared at him. 'It's a wonder we're not both dead! I insist on returning to London immediately.'

'I beg you to reconsider,' said Mr Wu agitatedly. I could see that he was almost as shaken up as we were. 'Please be assured that it will not happen again,' he went on. 'I will see that you are well guarded from now on.'

'What about you, Matthew?' asked Dad. 'Say the word and I'll have us on the first plane back to London.'

Up till now I'd been too busy to be scared, but now that it was all over the reaction hit me. I looked at the bullet-ridden, blood-soaked bodies of the Triad assassins and shuddered. I began to shiver and my legs felt unsteady.

'Let's think it over,' I said shakily. 'There may not be a flight, and even if there is, I don't think I can face another thirteen hours on a plane right now.' I looked again at the wrecked buggy and the bodies. 'It might be a good idea to get away from this spot and to somewhere more safe, though. They might have a back-up squad.'

'Yes, yes, of course, we shall leave immediately,' said Mr Wu.

He ushered us into the back of the limousine and sat down facing us. The driver hit the accelerator and we screeched away.

As we sped swiftly away from the airport Mr Wu said, 'I must apologise again on behalf of my government for this atrocious attack. That two honoured guests should be assaulted the moment they set foot in Hong Kong! It is intolerable!' He paused. 'You reacted very quickly, young man. You probably saved all our lives. How did you know those men were dangerous?'

There was no way I was going to tell him I'd seen a ghost, not yet anyway. I shrugged and looked blank. 'No idea. I just sensed it somehow, as soon as I saw them speeding towards us.'

Dad had been sitting there unusually silent for a moment, possibly because he was still in a state of shock. Like me, he was just beginning to realise how close we'd been to dying, and his reaction took the form of anger.

'It's a disgrace! Those Triad villains were expecting us – they must have been sent to kill us! I have a good mind to fly back to London at once!'

Part of me thought that was a very good idea.

Another part, the obstinate and curious part, wanted to know what was going on.

Why was I seeing ghosts?

Why were the Triads so eager to kill us?

And what was the connection between the two?

'Come on, Dad,' I said. 'If we survived the Mafia in Sicily, we can survive the Triads in Hong Kong.'

'That's a very different matter!'

'I don't know that it is,' I said. I turned to Mr Wu. 'I gather the two organisations are pretty similar?'

'That is so,' said Mr Wu sadly. 'Though if anything, the Triads are even more ruthless – and more powerful.'

The Triads, like the Mafia, he told us, started centuries ago. 'They began as private armies, raised by rich merchants to protect them against the oppression of the Chinese Emperor. In time they became a group of independent secret societies – and they turned to crime. Drugs, protection rackets, kidnapping, they control it all. They influence politics, business, even the police, not only in Hong Kong but in China itself.'

I nodded, thinking of Italy, where even the Prime Minister had been accused of Mafia connections.

'Chinese people live and work all over the world,' Mr Wu went on. 'Wherever we go, the

Triads follow. They are very strong in New York – and even in London!'

Dad was scowling blackly. I could see he was still thinking about telling Mr Wu to turn the car, take us back to the airport, and put us on the first available plane back to London.

I decided to try a bit of distraction. If only I could get him interested in what was going on . . .

'Mr Wu, Ms Alexander said you'd give us a full report about what happened at the site,' I said. 'Do you think you could do that now? The more we know, the easier it will be to see if we can help.'

Mr Wu produced a sheaf of flimsy papers from his breast pocket and studied them for a moment.

'Two days ago, approximately midnight Hong Kong time, there was a disturbance on the site,' he announced in his BBC tones. 'One of the night-watchmen was found dead with a knife-wound in the back.'

'Was the weapon found?'

Mr Wu studied his papers. 'Apparently not. At least, it is not mentioned here.'

'Sorry to interrupt,' I said. 'Please go on.'

'Close by was the unconscious body of the head night-watchman. He was half-buried by a pile of collapsed lumber, battered but not severely hurt.'

'Sounds simple enough,' said Dad grumpily. 'The first night-watchman surprised a gang of thieves and they killed him. The second arrived and they knocked him out and fled. I expect they knocked over the timber as they escaped.'

'A truly rational, Western-style explanation,' said Mr Wu. 'Unfortunately the head night-watchman tells a different story. He insists that he saw a ferocious and malignant ghost hovering over his unfortunate colleague's body. The ghost tried to kill him too – by hurling a pile of lumber at him with supernatural power.'

'Obviously the man's confused,' said Dad. 'Confused, or lying.'

'Why should he lie?'

Dad shrugged. 'Perhaps he was in league with the thieves. He killed his fellow watchman and made up the ghost story to cover his tracks.'

'It is possible, of course,' said Mr Wu slowly. 'But according to Mr Henderson, the site manager, the head night-watchman – he is known as Big Han, by the way – is a trusted employee with years of loyal service.' He sighed. 'In any event, his story is the one the workmen believe. They were already convinced that the site was haunted. Apparently the ghost had been seen a number of times before. This incident was simply too much for them. They refuse to return to work – which is why we need your help.'

'But why us?' asked Dad. 'Don't you have local experts in the paranormal field?'

'Unfortunately, we do not,' said Mr Wu. He looked a little embarrassed. 'Officially, you understand, we are a rationalist society, guided only by the thoughts of the late, revered Chairman Mao. In China, paranormal studies are politically incorrect.'

'I see your problem,' I said. 'It's hard to investigate something that doesn't officially exist.'

'If your authorities won't allow their own people to investigate the paranormal, what makes you think they'll let us do it?' asked Dad. 'That's if I decide to stay,' he added grimly.

'Officially, your visit will have no connection to events at the site,' said Mr Wu. 'As you know, you have been invited to deliver a lecture at the Hong Kong Space Museum – the invitation is quite genuine, of course – and afterwards to spend a few days in Hong Kong as the honoured guest of the Chinese Government. Naturally, we shall wish to show such a distinguished visitor our new projects – such as the harbour redevelopment.'

I could see Dad was tempted, but he went on

putting up resistance. 'Is all this really so important? It's only another building project after all.'

'The importance of the harbour project is – symbolic,' said Mr Wu. 'There are those of us who wish to bring China closer to the West. I am happy to count myself among them. But there are others who wish us to retreat into hostile isolation. The success – or failure – of the project is important to both sides.'

'But surely this ghost story nonsense will soon die down?' protested Dad.

Once again Mr Wu looked embarrassed. 'As to that – officially, we scorn the supernatural. Unofficially, many of us revere the spirits of our ancestors, and believe in the powers of the unseen world. Believe me, ghosts are very real in Hong Kong!'

The car sped on.

We crossed the bridge linking Lantau Island to Hong Kong, and before very long the bare island countryside was replaced by something very like New York's Manhattan Island. We were in the heart of the city, surrounded by big shops and towering skyscrapers. Traffic clogged the roads, and people, an incredible number of people, crowded the pavements. Most were Chinese, but there were a fair-sized minority of Europeans as well. They hustled along the pavements, clutching shopping bags, briefcases and mobile phones.

'The ones with two mobile phones are probably drug dealers,' said Mr Wu.

'All the British-style red postboxes have been painted green!' said Dad indignantly.

Mr Wu was discreetly silent.

Everyone seemed to be in a great hurry. Looking out of the window I saw glowing, magical-looking Chinese signs – and the familiar golden arches of McDonald's. There was even a Planet Hollywood. Nice to think I needn't go short of a good hamburger and fries.

The car began climbing steadily upwards.

'This is the Peak,' said Mr Wu, 'the most prestigious part of Hong Kong. We have put you in one of our finest hotels, the one always used for visiting diplomats and government guests.'

Dad sniffed, but his expression mellowed a little. There's nothing he likes better than a touch of luxury – particularly at someone else's expense.

We turned up a tree-lined street and into the driveway of what was obviously a very expensive hotel. As we drew up before the front steps a flock of flunkeys appeared to deal with our luggage.

Mr Wu ushered us into a vast marble-floored, chandelier-hung foyer. He sped us through the process of checking in, and soon we were all shown into a luxurious lift.

After shooting innumerable floors upwards we were installed in a large and luxurious two-bedroomed suite.

Mr Wu made sure we were comfortably settled.

'You will need time to rest and refresh yourselves after your terrible ordeal.' He paused. 'And afterwards, may I suggest we meet for lunch?'

Dad frowned. 'Wouldn't it be safer to stay in the hotel?'

'I assure you that full security arrangements will be in place,' said Mr Wu. 'The lunch is a business matter, of course; there are some people I wish you to meet. I should be most grateful if you would attend.'

Dad nodded. 'Very well.'

Mr Wu looked relieved. 'Excellent! If I collect you, say in two hours' time?'

I looked at my watch, now set to Hong Kong time. 'It's past midday already. Won't two hours make it a bit late for lunch?'

Mr Wu beamed. 'Not in Hong Kong. We Chinese are not so concerned with set mealtimes. We eat when we are hungry – and we are usually hungry! We shall have *dim sum*!'

'Excellent!' said Dad.

Mr Wu said, 'I have invited Mr Henderson to join us. He is site manager on the harbour project. Mr Chalmers from your embassy will attend as well. I am sorry to press you, but something tells me that time is short.'

Dad graciously agreed to the arrangements and Mr Wu bowed himself out.

I went over to the mini-bar and fished out a can of Coke, a quarter bottle of champagne and a glass. I handed the last two to Dad and went over to the big picture-window with my Coke.

There, far down below me, was Hong Kong, with the harbour in the distance.

What an amazing mixture the whole place was.

Rickshaws and limousines. Sailing junks and skyscrapers. Luxury shops and street stalls, East and West all jammed together on a tiny over-crowded island.

Not to mention murderous Triads – and a murderous Chinese ghost as well.

I remembered what Mr Wu had said about ghosts being very real in Hong Kong.

Just how real I was soon to find out . . .

Chapter Three

DEADLY CONFERENCE

Dad opened his mini-bottle of champagne, filled his glass, and came to join me at the window.

'I still think we ought to go straight home, Matthew,' he said. 'After all, when people start trying to kill you as soon as you get off the plane . . .'

I had to admit he had a point. The ruthless efficiency of the Triad attack had shaken me up too. But I'd got over most of the shock by now. For some reason I was more angry than frightened. And I was intrigued as well. I could still see that strange ghostly figure hurtling towards me, remember that sudden sensation of overwhelming dread.

Somehow Dad seemed to sense what I was thinking.

'How did you manage to react so quickly, there at the airport?' he asked curiously. 'You shouted the moment those men came in sight – for all you knew they might have been airport workers.'

'They were all carrying guns, for a start!'

'All right, security guards, then. How did you know they were going to attack us?'

For some reason I still didn't want to discuss my strange visions with anyone, even Dad.

Not yet, anyway.

'Call it a premonition,' I said. 'I just got this sudden sense of danger.'

'All the more reason for us to leave!'

'Maybe so. But I hate the idea of our being frightened off as soon as we arrive . . . That means the Triads have won.'

Dad nodded, and I could see he felt much the same way. If there's one thing he hates, it's people trying to bully or frighten him.

That goes for me too.

There was a tap on the door. I went and peered through the spy-hole gadget. I saw a distorted picture of a young Chinese man in a dark green uniform. He held up a badge to his side of the spy-hole. I saw the reassuring words 'Hong Kong Security'.

I opened the door.

'Captain Lee, gentlemen,' he said. 'I am in

charge of your security, under Mr Wu.'

Like Mr Wu himself, he spoke perfect English.

'I just wanted to reassure you that you will be well guarded at all times,' he went on. 'I have men in the corridor, and others throughout the hotel. We are used to looking after VIPs here. We shall also escort you to the restaurant for lunch with Mr Wu in exactly one hour and forty-five minutes' time. Please permit me to apologise for the shocking incident on your arrival.'

We thanked him and he went away.

'Mr Wu didn't waste any time,' I said as I closed the door.

Captain Lee's visit did something to reassure Dad about our safety, but he was still muttering about catching the next plane home.

'At least let's wait till after lunch,' I said. 'It would be rude to cry off now we've accepted the invitation.'

'I suppose so,' said Dad grudgingly. He's very hot on good manners.

He sank down in one of the luxurious armchairs, and I sat down as well. 'Anyway,' I said. 'We really ought to stay and help the Chinese Government – just to make up for all our bad behaviour back in the nineteenth century.'

'All what bad behaviour?' demanded Dad indignantly. 'Permit me to tell you, Matthew, that when we British ran Hong Kong it was a model colony. And there was far less crime. Nobody tried to shoot me all the other times I came!'

'Ah, but what about the way we got Hong Kong in the first place? Come on, Dad, even you've got to admit it was one of the dodgier episodes in the history of the British Empire.'

Dad thinks the late, lamented British Empire was a thoroughly Good Thing and the world was a far better place when most of the atlas was still coloured an imperial red.

Just as I'd expected he rose to the bait.

'Why was it "dodgy", as you put it?' he demanded indignantly. 'What are we supposed to have done to China and the Chinese?'

'How about dope-pushing?'

'Nonsense!'

'It's all too true, I'm afraid.'

I went on to give him the benefit of my research into Hong Kong history. 'Back in the early nineteenth century, the Chinese were selling us tea.'

'What's wrong with that? No doubt we paid handsomely for it! "Trade follows the flag", as they used to say!'

'Oh yes. But the trouble was, the Chinese insisted on our paying in silver. Tea was very popular – and so much silver was going out of England and into China that the English treasury was in danger of going bankrupt. We had to find something the Chinese wanted as much as we wanted tea. Guess what we found?'

'No doubt you'll tell me,' said Dad resignedly. I could see he was intrigued all the same.

'Opium!' I said. 'We sold the Chinese people opium, they paid for it in silver, and we used the silver to buy our tea.'

Dad couldn't help looking shocked, but he did his best to brazen it out. 'So everyone was happy?'

'Except the Emperor of China,' I said. 'For some reason he didn't fancy ruling over a nation of dope addicts. He tried to put a stop to the opium business, and there was a short, sharp war. We had bigger and better guns, and the Chinese lost. We got our hands on Hong Kong as part of the final peace treaty. Now – is that dodgy or what?'

If there's one thing Dad hates it's losing an argument. 'Moral standards were different in those days,' he said grumpily. 'Besides, we gave it back, didn't we?'

'Eventually!' Dad rose and stretched.

'Well, thank you for the history lesson, Matthew. As you say, it's obviously our duty to stay in Hong Kong and make amends!'

In a funny way, I think he meant it!

Mr Wu arrived promptly to collect us for lunch, escorting us out to the front of the hotel where the limousine was waiting.

I was glad to catch sight of Captain Lee in the background, accompanied by several armed security guards.

As we pulled away from the hotel there was an unmarked security car in front of us, and another behind.

The limousine drove us through crowded streets and stopped outside a large and glittering restaurant not very far from the hotel.

'The Happy Dragon,' said Mr Wu proudly. 'One of the finest restaurants in Hong Kong. Their *dim sum* is unsurpassed!'

Escorted by Captain Lee and some of his men we went inside. The restaurant was very large and very noisy, with an incredible number of tables. It was crowded with hundreds of people, most but not all of them Chinese, eating and drinking and chattering happily.

Waitresses in neat black dresses were pushing trolleys up and down the aisles, between the tables. The trolleys were piled high with lidded round wickerwork baskets. Every so often the waitresses stopped at one or other of the tables.

It looked a nice jolly place, but a nightmare from the point of view of security. For all I knew, all those happy eaters could be Triad assassins with Uzi machine-pistols hidden under their shirts.

I needn't have worried; Mr Wu had it all under control.

He led us across the restaurant, up a flight of stairs and into a small private dining-room. We went inside, leaving Captain Lee and his men to guard the door.

The room was ornately furnished, with scarlet and gold wall hangings, embroidered with dragons. Wide-open French windows looked out on to a little balcony. Below the balcony I caught a glimpse of a garden of exotic-looking plants.

Three people were sitting at the big round dining-table. They rose as we came in.

'Gentlemen, this is our distinguished visitor Professor Stirling, and his son Matthew,' said Mr Wu. He turned to us.

'You already know Major Chang.'

He introduced the other two men.

The first was a big, red-faced, red-headed man in sports shirt and slacks. His rolled-up sleeves showed massive brawny forearms.

'This is Mr Douglas Henderson, site manager,' said Mr Wu.

'Pleased to meet you,' said the big man. 'Call me Douggie.'

He had a handshake like a steel clamp and his voice had an unmistakable Australian twang.

The second man was tall and thin, with a high forehead, horn-rimmed glasses and wispy hair.

'Mr Austen Chalmers, from the British Embassy,' said Mr Wu.

Mr Chalmers held out a long thin hand and mumbled, 'Awfly pleased . . .'

Introductions over, we all sat down.

Mr Wu looked round the table. 'As we all know, there have been a number of problems with the harbour redevelopment project,' he said. 'Professor Stirling has been kind enough to offer his help.'

The two men looked politely baffled.

'We can discuss the matter later,' said Mr Wu. 'First, we shall eat. In China, nothing is more important than a good meal!'

He clapped his hands and a procession of waitresses wheeling trolleys came into the room.

Dim sum turned out to be an incredibly varied selection of Chinese delicacies – fish, chicken, prawns, pork, squid, and many more. The different dishes were cooked and served in a variety of ways and individually presented in round wickerwork baskets – the waitress came to your table, lifted the lids of each of the baskets and you pointed to what you wanted.

The baskets were piled up before you, and you ate with chopsticks from little china bowls.

Chinese white wine and Chinese tea accompanied the meal. It was all delicious and I had some of everything.

Well, almost everything.

I passed on the chicken feet which, not surprisingly, looked exactly like chicken feet – little piles of sad, brown, wrinkly claws in some kind of sauce.

Mr Wu assured me they were delicious.

I said I'd take his word for it.

There wasn't much conversation during the meal. Everyone was too busy eating. Major Chang, in particular, ate steadily, dish after dish without saying a word. Socially, he wasn't much of an asset.

There was a sudden buzzing sound and Major Chang took a mobile phone from his pocket, listened, and spoke briefly in Chinese. He stood up.

'You excuse me, gentlemen. I must return to the airport.'

'Is there a clue to the identity of those guilty of this morning's outrage?' asked Mr Wu.

'Possibly. I go and see.'

Major Chang bowed stiffly and left.

By now we were all more or less full and a little silence fell. It was Douggie Henderson who spoke up. 'I take it that you're some kind of business consultant, professor? What's your line exactly? Finance? Architecture? The psychology of industrial relations?'

Dad shook his head. 'I'm a space scientist.'

'Cripes, that's just what we need!' said Douggie Henderson disgustedly. 'A flaming astronaut! We gonna move the harbour project to outer space?'

For a moment I thought Dad would blow up, but he only grinned. 'I'm sorry, Mr Henderson, I'm afraid I misled you. I *used* to be a space scientist. My current field is paranormal research.'

'Going to lay our ghost for us, are you?'

'Perhaps.'

'I'm afraid the ghost is only the latest of our

problems,' murmured Mr Chalmers, the man from the embassy. 'A sort of supernatural last straw.'

Suddenly I saw something on the other side of the table.

A tall, glowing form in the shape of an old man in Chinese robes.

He had a stern, angry face with long drooping moustaches and burning red eyes. He was glaring furiously at me.

Once again, I had the feeling the ghost was trying to tell me something.

The apparition raised a skinny, claw-like hand and pointed towards the door. All at once I had the same overwhelming sense of terror, of fear and approaching danger that I'd felt at the airport.

The ghostly figure faded away. I shuddered . . .

Dad must have caught my expression of horror. 'Matthew, what on earth's the matter? You look as if you've seen a ghost!'

If only he knew!

Before I could answer, a waiter came into the room carrying a wickerwork basket. It was round, like the others, but very much bigger.

'I really don't think we need any more food,' said Mr Wu, waving him away.

The head waiter's villainous-looking face – there was something lopsided about it – was wreathed in a beaming smile.

'But this is special dish, gentlemen,' he announced. 'Special pudding, for dessert. Called *bombe surprise*! With compliments of management. Chef will be most offended if you do not try it!'

He leaned forward to put the big basket on the table. The sleeve of his robe fell back and I saw the dragon tattoo on his wrist.

I moved without even thinking, grabbed the basket and hurled it through the open French windows.

Everyone stared at me as if I'd gone mad.

'Matthew, what the devil . . . ?' said Dad. He looked round the room. 'I'm sorry, gentlemen, the boy's been under some strain.'

Then we heard the shattering explosion from outside the open French windows . . .

Chapter Four

AFTERMATH OF TERROR

There was panic and pandemonium after that.

Everyone at the table jumped up in alarm. Looking round, I saw that the head waiter had vanished.

Captain Lee's men ran into the room, waving guns.

We could hear terrified screams and angry shouts of alarm from the main restaurant below.

I went over to the French windows and looked over the balcony. Everyone followed, crowding round and looking over my shoulder.

There in the garden below was a small, still-smoking crater. The bomb had made a very nasty mess of a handsome flower-bed.

I went back into the room and collapsed into my chair. Dad leaned over me and grabbed me by my shoulders. 'Are you all right, Matthew?'

As a matter of fact I wasn't. My knees felt weak and my heart was pounding and I found it difficult to breathe.

I drew a deep breath and did my best to put a brave face on things. 'I'm all right, I think.' I grinned feebly. 'More frightened than hurt, as they say.'

'Matthew, you are the hero of the hour!' said Mr Wu. 'That bomb would have killed everyone in this room. You saved all our lives!'

'I was mainly worrying about my own!' I said.

Douggie Henderson and Mr Chalmers crowded round and added their congratulations.

Mr Henderson said, 'Good on you, sport, you played a blinder!'

Mr Chalmers murmured, 'Awfly good show.'

I did my best to look suitably modest.

Even Dad joined in the chorus of praise. 'Yes, indeed, well done, Matthew!' He looked curiously at me. 'You reacted very quickly – again. What on earth made you suspect there was a bomb in that basket? Another premonition?'

Once again I didn't want to talk about the ghost – certainly not in front of a room full of strangers.

'I saw the dragon tattoo on the man's wrist when he put down the basket.'

Captain Lee came over in time to hear what I was saying. He looked curiously at me. 'How could you be so sure? Many people here in Hong Kong have tattoos.'

'That particular design of dragon is a Triad sign,' I said. 'Major Chang showed us a larger version on the back of that man at the airport – the one he shot.' I turned to Mr Wu. 'You remember, don't you?'

Mr Wu nodded. 'Yes indeed. First the airport – now this!'

Captain Lee said, 'The man who brought the basket was a last-minute replacement for their regular head waiter, who fell mysteriously ill at the last moment.' He smiled grimly. 'I rather imagine someone from the Triad told him it would be better for his health to be ill today!'

Captain Lee looked around the room. 'Did anyone see what this new head waiter looked like?'

Nobody seemed to have registered the man at all.

Nobody but me.

I was feeling less shaky now, and made an effort to pull myself together.

'I got a good look at one side of his face as he leaned past me to put down the basket,' I said. 'I think there was something funny about it . . .'

'Funny how?' asked Captain Lee sharply.

I struggled to remember. 'His ear! The lower bit was missing . . .'

'Half-Ear Huang,' said Captain Lee instantly. 'The rest of the ear was removed by a rival with a meat-cleaver, when Huang was still a humble soldier of the Triad. I'll put out a general order to pick him up.'

He summoned a subordinate and fired off a string of orders in Chinese. The man saluted and hurried away.

'Not that it will do any good,' said Captain Lee gloomily. 'He'll be well away by now. He'll go into hiding somewhere, here in Hong Kong, or Macau, maybe even in China; they've got contacts everywhere.' He frowned. 'It's odd, though. Huang's fairly senior in the Triad these days. Not the man you'd expect to carry out this kind of job himself.'

'Perhaps they were trying to wipe out this morning's failure,' said Mr Wu. He looked thoughtfully at me and Dad. 'What I don't understand is why you are so important to them.'

'I'm not sure we are,' I said.

'After all that's happened!' spluttered Dad. 'Come now, Matthew!'

'This morning's attack could have been aimed just as much at Major Chang and Mr Wu,' I argued. 'And as for this one – you said yourself, that bomb would have killed everyone in this room. They could have been after any or all of us. I think it's all to do with the harbour project. Everyone at this lunch is concerned with it.'

'I think you may be right,' said Douggie Henderson. 'The project has been nothing but trouble from the beginning. Endless delays over licences, permits, permissions – in China these things always take time. But this was worse than anything I've ever had to deal with before.'

'I can only apologise,' said Mr Wu. 'Bureaucracy is the same everywhere, I fear.'

'Things were just as bad when we actually started work,' Douggie went on. 'Building materials arriving late, sometimes not arriving at all. Or the wrong materials delivered. Equipment breaking down, absentee workforce . . . We even had an entire shipment of explosives stolen.' A thought struck him. 'Strewth, maybe they were trying to blow me up with me own dynamite!'

'The Triad must be behind all this,' said Dad. 'After all, they're the ones who tried to kill us as soon as we arrived. Now they've tried again –

presumably because we were coming to help you.'

'I guess the Triad must be in it somewhere,' said Douggie Henderson. 'But I can't see why! Usually they like to see these big projects go ahead, so they can get their cut. They don't try to sabotage them. Where's the profit in that?'

'What about the ghost?' I asked.

'You'd have to ask Big Han about that,' said Douggie. 'He's the one who saw it last. He turned out because he heard robbers on the site and this ghost popped up and tried to kill him.'

Dad brought the discussion to an end. 'Well, whoever the Triads are after, we certainly seem to be pretty high on their list of enemies,' he said. 'I am sorry, Mr Wu, but I must insist on leaving Hong Kong at once. I'm willing to tackle ghosts, but not gangsters. I'm not prepared to endanger the life of myself and my son any longer. We've had two very near misses. I don't want to give the Triads a chance to make it third time lucky.'

I'd been afraid he would take this attitude.

To be fair, the old boy is brave enough. If he'd been on his own he'd probably have stayed on and defied the Triads to do their worst. It was my skin he was worried about – and I didn't want to go. Quite why, I wasn't sure.

It's not that I wasn't scared. I was terrified. I'm no keener on being shot at or bombed than anyone else.

But despite my fears, I had a strange feeling that my being in Hong Kong was important, that there was something I had to do.

It was all connected with the fierce apparition that had appeared at both assassination attempts.

And for some strange reason I just *had* to visit that site. It was a compulsion . . .

'I greatly regret your decision, professor, but I understand completely,' Mr Wu was saying. 'We shall return to the hotel and I will put your travel arrangements in hand at once.'

'Thank you,' said Dad. 'The first available flight to London, if you please.'

A cunning plan was forming in my mind. 'Hang on a minute,' I said.

Dad gave me his 'I have spoken' look. 'I'm sorry, Matthew, I won't listen to any arguments. We're leaving Hong Kong as soon as possible.'

I knew better than to try to talk him into changing his mind. Not yet, anyway – and not directly.

'I'm not talking about not leaving,' I said. I gave

him an offended look. 'If you'll allow me to finish?'

As I said, Dad's very keen on good manners. 'I'm sorry, Matthew,' he said stiffly. 'Please go on.'

I turned to Mr Wu. 'How soon do you think you'll be able to get us on a plane to London?'

'As I remember, the last direct flight leaves late tonight. I fear that by now it will be fully booked. An important diplomatic conference has just finished and many distinguished foreign visitors are on their way home. I will do my best for you, but it may be necessary to wait until tomorrow.'

'Then get us on a plane to anywhere today,' said Dad angrily. 'Macau, Moscow, Beijing, I don't care.'

Mr Wu looked worried. 'I do not think that is advisable. It will be hard for me to ensure your protection.'

'You haven't been doing very well up to now!' retorted Dad.

'But Mr Wu's right, Dad,' I said. 'You heard Captain Lee – the Triads have connections everywhere. If we go dashing around all over the Orient we'll be setting ourselves up as targets. It's just not logical.'

Dad is even keener on logic than he is on good manners. 'Very well, then,' he said. 'Back to

London, please, Mr Wu. And as soon as possible.'

Before Mr Wu could reply, I said, 'And that isn't going to be before late this evening at the earliest, right? And possibly not then?'

'So?' said Dad suspiciously.

I produced my bright idea. 'So instead of skulking in our hotel rooms, let's use the time we have to take a look at the harbour development site. At least our time here won't have been completely wasted. Maybe we can give some advice.'

Dad shook his head. 'It isn't safe.'

'If anything it's safer,' I argued. 'The hotel's where they'll expect to find us, not the site. Captain Lee and his men can come as well, and I'm sure Mr Henderson will show us around.'

'My pleasure, sport,' said Henderson. 'And I told you, call me Douggie.'

'I'll come too, if I may,' said Chalmers. 'It's just possible I may be able to be of assistance. I know a little about the harbour area. The history of old Hong Kong is a hobby of mine.'

It took quite a while to persuade Dad, but he gave way at last. I think it was my reference to our 'skulking in our hotel rooms' that did it.

We Stirlings do not skulk!

Mr Wu said, 'I will make immediate enquiries

about your travel arrangements. I will follow you down to the site as soon as I have definite news. If necessary, I will have your luggage packed and sent on, and you can go to the airport direct from the site.'

Dad allowed himself to be persuaded. 'Thank you,' he said. 'I'm sorry to give you so much trouble, but you understand how I feel.'

'Of course, of course,' said Mr Wu soothingly, and moved away.

'Don't worry, professor, we will take good care of you and your son,' said Captain Lee. He smiled ruefully. 'Oh, I know we haven't done too well so far, but now we shall be extra vigilant. Security has been doubled.'

I left them talking, and hurried after Mr Wu. I managed to catch him at the door.

'Mr Wu!'

'Yes, Mr Stirling?'

'I hope you will forgive my father for being – difficult. It's not that he's afraid for himself . . .'

'No, no,' said Mr Wu. 'He is worried about the threat to the life of Number One Son. He cares for you very much. And you for him.'

I suddenly felt myself coming over all British. 'Well, yes, I suppose so. The thing is . . .'

'Yes, Mr Stirling?'

'I myself am very keen to stay on in Hong Kong and give any help we can. I don't feel we've had a proper chance to get to grips with the problem.'

'Your father's attitude makes things very difficult for you,' said Mr Wu. 'Of course, the good son must always obey his father.'

'Of course,' I agreed. 'Only . . .'

'Only what, Mr Stirling?'

I looked him straight in the eye. 'If you were unable to book us on a direct flight to London until tomorrow – or even the next day . . .'

'Your father would be very angry.'

'At first. But I'm sure he would bow to the inevitable. After all, what else could he do?'

Mr Wu gave me a thoughtful look. 'He would not, perhaps, attempt to check up on the travel situation, or make his own arrangements?'

'Dad?' I shook my head. 'He's not exactly the practical type – and he's used to having things done for him. If you tell him the flights are all booked . . .'

Mr Wu shook his head. 'Dear me!'

'What?'

'I thought it was only we Chinese who were supposed to be cunning and devious!'

'I've no idea what you mean,' I said innocently.

'Well, I must get on with making your travel arrangements,' said Mr Wu. 'But I am not too optimistic. This is a *very* busy time of year!'

He hurried away.

I went back to join the others.

'What was all that about?' asked Dad suspiciously.

'All what?'

'Your chat with Mr Wu.'

'I was just apologising for you,' I said. 'Even if we can't stay and help, there's no point ruining Anglo–Chinese relations.'

Dad gave me an indignant glare. But before he could protest, he was interrupted by Douggie Henderson. 'Right, everybody ready? Your blokes all set, Captain Lee?'

Surrounded by bodyguards, we made our way through the still-agitated crowd in the restaurant and out to the waiting transport.

We all piled into the roomy limousine – me, Dad, Mr Chalmers and Douggie Henderson. With security cars in front and behind we drove away from the restaurant.

We drove off the Peak and through the crowded Central district. It was instant New York again –

eighty-storey skyscrapers, luxury shops, flashing neon signs . . .

A few minutes later we were in a different world.

Narrow twisting streets, ramshackle buildings . . . There were markets and street stalls and crowds of pedestrians and cyclists, almost all of them Chinese.

We came out on to the stunning vista of Hong Kong harbour – sparkling water, junks crowded along the shoreline, green and white Star ferry-boats chugging to and fro, distant hills looming beyond.

'Tanka and Hoklo boat people live on those junks,' said Mr Chalmers diffidently. 'In the old days many of them were born, worked, lived and died afloat, never coming ashore. Things are changing now.'

We turned left and drove along the waterfront, through an area that became steadily more run-down. Finally we arrived at a huge wooden fence barring our way. There was a massive wooden gate, flanked by two armed security guards.

'This is where the project really starts,' said Douggie as the cars drew up.

We all got out and stood looking up at the fence.

'We've sectioned off a chunk of the most run-down bit of the harbour,' said Douggie. 'We're clearing out the old shacks and rebuilding from scratch.'

'Luxury flats for wealthy yuppies?' asked Dad.

'Certainly not!'

'That's what seems to happen in London.'

'Not here,' said Douggie indignantly. 'We're going for a balanced district – good low-cost housing, shops, factories, offices. Jobs and places to live.'

Dad saw that he was sincere. 'I'm sorry, Mr Henderson.'

Douggie grinned. 'That's all right, sport. I'm not pretending to be some kind of do-gooder. Business is business, and we're here to make a profit. But those buildings we're clearing out, although they may be picturesque, they're also death-traps. They're fire risks, insanitary, riddled with disease. Life will be a lot better for a lot of hard-up people in Hong Kong if this project goes ahead.'

And if we can find out what's holding it up, I thought, in whatever few hours we've got left.

We went through the gate into a muddy waste-land dotted with earth-moving machines and piles of building materials.

'Looks like hell, doesn't it?' said Douggie cheerfully. 'Got a long way to go yet.'

Over to the right was a low hill overlooking the harbour. There was a building on top of it, a ruined Chinese pagoda.

'What's that?' I asked.

'A bit we haven't got round to clearing just yet,' said Douggie. 'We were just getting stuck in there when the trouble started. There's an old ruin on top, used to be some kind of temple. Come along to the site office. I'll organise a cuppa and show you the plans.'

As the others followed him away, I felt a sudden chill. I turned and looked back at the desolate ruined temple.

I saw a glowing, white-robed figure standing outside the distant temple, watching me.

Now I knew why I'd felt so compelled to visit the site.

It was the home of my personal Chinese ghost . . .

Chapter Five

THE HAUNTED TEMPLE

Frightened as I was, I wasn't surprised by the sight of the apparition. Somehow I'd been expecting it. I'd felt its presence growing ever stronger as we'd got closer to the site.

Now I knew why. The ruined temple was its home.

The big question was, what did it want of me?

As I watched, the ghost faded slowly away.

I turned and followed the others.

The site office was a big, sparsely-furnished wooden hut.

It held a desk, a few chairs, a long wooden table and some basic kitchen facilities. Maps and charts were pinned along the walls. There was a bunk bed in the corner. I guessed that Douggie Henderson sometimes spent the night on site. He was the sort of man who'd live with his work.

Douggie put on an electric kettle and made an enormous pot of incredibly strong tea. He produced a packet of sugar and a bottle of milk, fished out an assortment of cups and mugs and poured tea for everyone.

He took a swig from his mug and sighed with relief. 'Keeps me going, plenty of good strong char! Now, what can I tell you?'

Suddenly everyone was looking at me.

'It was your idea to come here, Matthew,' said Dad gently.

My mind was still full of the apparition at the temple. It took me a moment to gather my thoughts. 'Ah, right,' I said. 'Well, just tell us what's been happening. Anything strange or unusual. And about the ghost, of course.'

Douggie took another swig of tea. 'Not all that much to tell, really. I told you all the troubles we had getting started?'

I nodded. 'I gather that was just normal, everyday stuff. Nothing – supernatural?'

'I'm not so sure,' said Douggie gloomily. 'If ever a job had a curse on it . . . Nothing seemed to go right! Delayed permits, missing materials and supplies. Then there were the machinery breakdowns – I'm pretty sure some of that was

56

sabotage, but I could never prove it. Took us for ever to get started. Still, we did get started in the end, put in a fair bit of work clearing the site. Then the ghost turned up.'

'What was it like?'

'Never saw it myself. Far as I can make out from the blokes, it's a skinny old Chinese feller in a white robe. Very fierce and angry-looking, with glowing red eyes.'

It was a pretty disrespectful description, but it matched what I'd seen at the airport and in the restaurant – and now right here on the site.

'And what did the ghost do?' I asked.

Douggie shrugged. 'Floated in the air, glowed in the dark, all the usual spooky stuff. Only the night-watchmen saw it at first. Then word got about, and it started appearing in the daytime. Before long half the workforce had seen it – or thought they had! Absenteeism shot right up. You know how these things spread around.'

'We do indeed,' said Dad. 'That's the whole problem with paranormal investigation. There's always a confusing cloud of rumour and superstition and imagination.'

'But sometimes there's a silver lining of truth,' I said.

'If you're lucky,' said Dad.

'We've been lucky quite a few times,' I reminded him.

I turned back to Douggie. 'Go on about the ghost. What did you do about it?'

'Nothing really. What could I do? It didn't seem to be doing any real harm and I reckoned the whole thing would die away in time.'

'And did it?'

'Well, it was starting to. Everyone kind of got used to it, I suppose. Absenteeism went back to normal and the work got going again. Then there was the stabbing.'

'Tell us about that.'

'Well, I've only got it at second-hand. I was away that night. Big Han, my head watchman, was doing the rounds when he spotted something. He went to take a look and found one of his men dead, stabbed in the back, with the ghost hovering over him. Next thing Han knew, he was knocked out by falling lumber. Next day the story was all over the site. The ghost had stabbed the night-watchman and tried to kill Big Han by chucking a pile of lumber at him. The men ran away in droves, and most of them stayed away.'

'So the work's at a standstill?'

'Completely. The company's talking to the workmen's leaders, trying to raise a new workforce, but it doesn't look good. And we're getting no help from the new Hong Kong authorities either.'

'Have you considered some kind of exorcism?' asked Dad.

'A ceremony by some local priest, that sort of thing. It might reassure your workmen. It might even lay the ghost!'

'I thought about that,' said Douggie. 'I had the same problem in South America once, a haunted site. I persuaded the local shaman to perform a ghost-chasing ceremony and everything was fine.'

'Why didn't you do the same thing here?'

'The new authorities wouldn't have it. No place for ignorance and superstition on Chinese territory.'

'That's right,' I said. 'Mr Wu said the same thing. Ghosts have no official existence in the new China!'

'Tell that to my workmen!' said Douggie bitterly.

I thought for a moment. 'The man who was stabbed – was the knife still in his back?'

'No, I don't think so.'

'Was any kind of weapon found near by?'

'Not as far as I know.' Douggie grinned uneasily. 'Maybe it was a ghost-dagger, and faded away with the ghost!'

I looked at Dad. 'What do you think?'

'I suppose it's as good a theory as any!'

'I've never heard of a supernatural weapon leaving a real wound,' I said. 'Ghosts sometimes frighten people to death, but they don't shoot them or stab them.'

Dad shrugged. 'Maybe it's different in Hong Kong.'

'Everything's different in Hong Kong,' said Mr Chalmers quietly. It was the first time he'd spoken, and we all looked at him in surprise.

'Well, that's the lot,' said Douggie. 'You're the expert, professor. What do you make of it?'

'Not much,' said Dad frankly. 'I'm like the police in a Sherlock Holmes story – baffled. What about you, Matthew?'

'It's an odd sort of mixture,' I said.

Douggie frowned. 'How do you mean? What's a mixture?'

'All your troubles – a mixture of the natural and the supernatural. I've never heard of a ghost that holds up work permits, steals material, sabotages machinery – and stabs people in the back!'

'All that could be the work of the Triads,' Dad pointed out. 'But then there's the ghost!'

'Yes,' I said. 'Then there's the ghost.' I turned to

Douggie. 'This head watchman of yours . . .'

'Big Han? What about him?'

'I suppose he's still in hospital?'

'Not a bit of it. He's one of the few back at work,' Douggie laughed. 'Takes more than a pile of lumber on the head to worry Big Han.'

'Is he here now?'

'Yeah, he asked to be put on day shift. Less chance of meeting the ghost again, I guess!'

'I'd very much like to talk to him.'

'Sure, he won't be far. I'll give him a shout.'

Which was exactly what he did.

Douggie went to the door, opened it and bellowed, 'Han, where are you? Get yourself over here!'

A few minutes later, one of the biggest men I've ever seen came into the hut. He wore rough work-clothes and he had a craggy, impassive face. He stood in the doorway, towering over all of us, even the massive Douggie.

'Han, this young man wants you to tell him about seeing the ghost. The one that tried to kill you.'

Big Han stared blankly at me and didn't speak.

I went over to Douggie and whispered, 'He does speak English?'

'Ah, well, that could be a problem, sport. Usually

he speaks it pretty well; we can usually talk about the job. But then again, if he doesn't *want* to talk to you – well, his English might just suddenly vanish!'

Mr Chalmers from the embassy spoke up for the second time. 'Perhaps I can help. I speak reasonably good Cantonese.'

'Please,' I said. 'I'd be very grateful. Will you ask him exactly what he saw? Ask if he thinks the ghost killed the night-watchman, and if it really tried to kill him.'

Chalmers let out a stream of fluent Cantonese. Big Han answered Chalmers' questions in a low, guttural voice.

When he'd finished Chalmers said, 'He says he thought the ghost had tried to kill him at first, but now he has thought about it he has changed his mind. He doesn't believe the ghost killed the other night-watchman either. He thinks the man was killed by Triad thieves. And the ghost didn't try to kill him. He thinks more Triad thieves pushed the timber pile on to him. Somehow the ghost moved him out of the way of the falling timber. He says it saved his life.'

Han's words confirmed an idea of my own. In spite of its terrifying appearance, I wasn't sure that the ghost was entirely malignant.

The ghost I'd seen had saved my life, just as it had saved Big Han's. Stabbing people in the back didn't seem to fit somehow.

'Ask him if he's had any contact with the ghost since then.'

Once again Chalmers spoke, and Big Han replied.

'He says that he hasn't – and that even if the ghost has saved his life he still would avoid another encounter!'

We tried a few more questions and answers, but that was pretty well all Han had to tell us.

Chalmers thanked him and sent him on his way.

Douggie Henderson was delighted. 'That could be really useful,' he said. 'If I spread that story, and Big Han backs it up, we'll be back to a benevolent spook again. Maybe they'll come back to work. Thanks a lot, Matt, maybe you've been some help after all.'

There was a tap on the door and Mr Wu came in. He bowed to my father and said, 'To my regret, there are no seats on flights to London before noon tomorrow. I am so sorry.'

Mr Wu and I avoided catching each other's eye.

Dad took the news surprisingly well. The fact that nobody had tried to shoot us or blow us up for some time seemed to have calmed him down a little.

'Have you made any progress here?' asked Mr Wu.

We told him of our conversation with Big Han and he agreed that the new slant on the ghost report might be useful.

Douggie looked at his watch. 'If you blokes want a look round the site, we'd better get moving.'

We trudged out into the muddy wasteland and Captain Lee and his men closed in protectively. As we walked around the site Douggie painted a glowing picture of its glorious future – if he could only get back to work.

There wasn't really a lot to look at on the deserted site, and the tour was soon over.

'Can we take a look at the ruined temple?' I asked.

'Sure, if you like. There's nothing much to see.'

We trudged up the little hill and stood outside the ruined building, looking over the harbour. Despite its dilapidated state, I recognised it as the temple I'd seen in my dream.

'Do you know anything about this place?' I asked.

'Not a thing,' said Douggie cheerfully. 'That's

one advantage of the new set-up – I don't have to worry about it.'

'How do you mean?'

'Well, if this was in Europe I'd have archaeologists and environmentalists climbing all over me, screaming blue murder if I touched a single tile. Even here in Hong Kong, in the old days . . . This new lot don't seem to care if I bulldoze the entire temple tomorrow.'

I felt a sudden chill, a sense of dread, and a wave of fierce anger. It was all surging up out of the temple . . .

'Maybe somebody cares,' I said.

Douggie laughed. 'Like the ghost, you mean? You reckon that's why it's kicking up?'

'Many a true word spoken in jest, Douggie!'

Douggie didn't seem very impressed. Obviously he'd felt nothing. 'Be getting dark pretty soon,' he said. 'Maybe our friendly spook will put in a special appearance for us.'

I looked around. There were lots of us on the bare windswept hill – me, Dad, Chalmers, Mr Wu and Douggie himself. Not to mention Captain Lee and his ever-vigilant security guards hovering close by.

'I doubt if the ghost will turn up now,' I said.

'Not unless it likes making public appearances before large crowds. It's a ghost, not a politician – and most ghosts are pretty shy.'

I turned to Dad. 'You know what we ought to do?'

'What?'

'Spend the night here. That's what you'd do if you were ghost-hunting in a haunted house. Why not on a haunted building site?'

'Out of the question,' said Dad firmly. 'Forget it, Matthew. We're going straight back to the hotel and staying in our suite under guard till we catch our plane. And I want to be back at that hotel before dark!'

'All right, all right,' I said wearily. 'It was just an idea.'

I'd known all along he would never agree.

All the same, it was incredibly frustrating being so close, and being unable to investigate further.

As we walked down the hill, Mr Chalmers came up beside me. 'If you really want to know more about the temple, I may be able to help,' he murmured. 'I have some old books on local history at home. As it happens, I live on the Peak myself, quite close to your hotel. It's almost on your way. I'd be happy to offer you a glass of sherry. Well, not you precisely, I'd have to find you some more suitable drink, but perhaps your father . . .'

He waffled on confusedly for a bit, and I cut him off as politely as I could. 'Thanks,' I said. 'We accept with pleasure.'

'Are you sure your father . . .?'

'Leave him to me,' I said. I hurried on to catch up with Dad, who was talking to Captain Lee and Mr Wu.

'Dad, Mr Chalmers from the embassy has invited us both for drinks,' I said. 'I think we ought to accept.'

Dad frowned, but before he could say anything I turned to Captain Lee. 'Can you handle the security OK?'

Captain Lee beamed. 'Most certainly. I am familiar with Mr Chalmers' residence. It is a safe apartment in a good area; it will be easy to guard.'

'I don't think the risk is too great,' said Mr Wu. 'I have taken the liberty of cancelling your lecture at the space museum, professor, and of announcing that you are leaving Hong Kong immediately.'

'There you are then, Dad,' I said cheerfully. 'The Triads will be convinced they've frightened you off. Maybe they'll be content with that and won't bother you any more.'

Dad frowned. I could see that he didn't greatly care for the phrase 'frightened you off'.

As I'd hoped, it helped to get him to agree to visit Chalmers.

'Very well, Matthew,' he said. 'Tell Mr Chalmers we accept his invitation with pleasure.'

I grinned. 'I already have,' I said.

We were walking out of the gates when suddenly I felt another eerie chill.

Somehow I sensed a wave of fierce anger – combined with an underlying despair. Once again, it was coming from the temple.

Falling back a little, I turned and saw a tall, white-robed figure standing in the temple doorway. Even from this distance I could feel the glare of its red eyes . . .

I made a desperate, last-minute attempt to communicate with the angry ghost.

'Look, I'm sorry, I don't know what you want. And even if I did, I just can't help you, they're taking me away from Hong Kong tomorrow!'

Dad turned round. 'Sorry, Matthew, did you say something?'

I hadn't realised I'd spoken out loud. I shook my head. 'No, nothing . . .'

I hurried after the others.

Chapter Six

HAUNTED

Mr Chalmers lived in a big, old-fashioned apartment in a big, old-fashioned building on the Peak, not far from our hotel.

The nice old Chinese lady who let us in was obviously Mr Chalmers' housekeeper. Even Captain Lee didn't seem to think that she might be a Triad killer in disguise. He checked out the rest of the flat and pronounced it secure. Then he left us to our drinks, assuring us that there would be guards outside the door and around the building.

Chalmers showed us into a book-lined study.

The housekeeper served Dad and Chalmers a decanter of sherry on a silver tray, and produced diet Coke for me.

Chalmers caught Dad's disapproving look. 'I sometimes have visitors from the American

Embassy,' he said apologetically. 'I keep it for them, it's all they seem to drink!'

Dad sipped his sherry appreciatively. 'They don't know what they're missing.'

Mr Chalmers produced a massive leather-bound volume from his shelves and passed it over to me. 'I think you might find this of interest,' he murmured. 'Chapter seven, if my memory serves. You'll find that armchair quite comfortable.'

He switched on a reading-lamp beside the chair and left me to it.

While Dad and Chalmers sipped sherry and discussed the good old British-rule days in Hong Kong, I turned the pages of the book.

It was a history of old Hong Kong. Chapter seven dealt with the harbour area.

There was mention of a temple – well, lots of temples actually; Hong Kong is full of them. But one in particular caught my interest. It was on the far edge of the harbour, in the area now covered by Douggie's building site.

On a low hill overlooking the harbour there stands the temple to Master Jiang Shing, a famous judge of the Tang dynasty. Jiang Shing was famous for his many virtues. These included a ferocious dedication to justice,

*and an ability to predict the future. He was also famed
for his care and protection of the harbour folk and boat
people.*

*When Master Jiang Shing took office, the harbour
folk were being terrorised by pirates, forerunners of
today's Triads. It is recorded that when a pirate captain
tried to kill him, Jiang Shing wrested the weapon away
from him and stabbed the pirate to death with his own
dagger.*

*Subsequently, Jiang Shing and his Imperial police
wiped out the bandits with ruthless efficiency, behead-
ing a hundred of them in one day on the harbourside.*

*After this, Jiang Shing was known as The Execu-
tioner. He was greatly feared. But although he could be
stern and cruel, he was never unjust. He was also
greatly respected, even loved by the humble boat people.*

*The temple of Jiang Shing is also his tomb, and it is
rumoured that his ghost still hovers protectively by the
temple, watching over the interests of the area and the
humble harbour folk and boat people he protected in life.*

*Sadly, the little temple is now neglected, worshippers
preferring the larger, more ornate temples such as Man
Mo and the triple-halled Pak Tai . . .*

There was a portrait of Jiang Shing on the opposite page.

He was a very tall, stern-faced man in Chinese robes. In the picture his hair and long moustaches were still black. His face was filled with strength and wisdom, and the eyes were ablaze with life.

He looked very familiar . . .

Was it possible that Jiang Shing's ghost was still watching over his beloved harbour?

Well, of course it was.

Big Han had seen him, and the ghost had saved his life. I'd seen him myself, and he'd saved *my* life – twice!

I still felt that he wanted my help in some way. Now he was angry with me because I wouldn't give it. But what could I possibly do in the little time I had left? Tomorrow we were leaving Hong Kong . . .

I turned to the front page of the book and looked up the publication date. It was nineteen hundred. Jiang Shing's temple had been looking neglected a hundred years ago. No wonder it was in such a bad way today. Now what was left of it was due for demolition by Douggie's bulldozers. And there wasn't a thing I could do about it.

Dad's indignant voice brought me back to the present. '. . . and they've actually painted all your nice red postboxes that turgid green!'

'Did it the day after they took over,' said Chalmers. 'Mind you, they didn't use very good quality paint. With lots of them the green's already wearing off, and you can see the red underneath.'

'Aha!' said Dad triumphantly.

I closed the book and stood up.

'Find anything interesting?' asked Chalmers.

'Very much so,' I said. 'The temple on the site is the tomb of someone called Jiang Shing. I think it all ought to be preserved, even restored if possible. That might put an end to the haunting at least.'

'I'll tell Douggie Henderson,' said Chalmers. 'But I don't think archaeological restoration is really one of his main interests!'

I remembered Douggie's attitude back on the site. 'I'm afraid you're right.'

There was a bit more polite chitchat and we said our goodbyes. I was genuinely sorry, I liked Chalmers a lot.

Captain Lee was waiting outside, and he and his men took us back to the hotel. He said Mr Wu had sent us a message that our flights were confirmed. He and Captain Lee would escort us to the airport in the morning.

Captain Lee saw us safely into our suite, first checking for hidden Triad thugs.

'If you wish to dine out, please inform me and I will provide an escort,' he said. 'However, it would simplify matters if you would agree to eat here in the hotel.'

'We're going to eat right here in our suite,' said Dad grimly. 'We've had more than enough local colour and exotic excitement for one day.'

He realised he was being bossy – something I've often had to tell him about – and turned to me. 'I assume that suits you, Matthew? You're not craving a visit to some local discotheque?'

He's got a weird sense of humour sometimes.

I gave him a withering glance that was very nearly as good as one of his own. 'Dinner in the room will suit me fine. Or even a sandwich. I'm still pretty full of *dim sum*. But check that room service really is just room service, will you please, Captain Lee? We had a bit of trouble in Cairo once.'

'I assure you the door will be guarded at all times. Nobody will enter or leave this room without rigorous scrutiny.'

We dialled room service and ordered beer and beef sandwiches for Dad and a Coke and ham sandwiches for me. Supervised by Captain Lee, a hotel waiter delivered them soon afterwards – unaccompanied by bombs, knives or guns.

We took the food to a table by the window and ate looking out over Hong Kong harbour.

After a while Dad said, 'Are you very disappointed, Matthew?'

'A bit,' I confessed. 'Nothing attempted, nothing done . . . Do you realise, this is our first failure?'

'You're not being fair to yourself, Matthew. We did all we could, or rather you did. Your suggestion of getting Big Han to tell everyone that the ghost saved his life was genuinely useful.'

'Maybe,' I said. 'But it's not much of an achievement, is it?'

'Do you really think preserving and restoring that temple will end the hauntings?' asked Dad.

'I think there's a chance. Desecrating sacred sites is never a very good idea.'

'What about all their other problems? The delays and the sabotage?'

'I'm still not sure. I think there may be a mixture of reasons for all their problems, some natural, some paranormal. We never really got a chance to find out, did we?'

'Well, I'm sorry,' said Dad. 'Under the circumstances, I can't see any alternative to going straight back home. We're way out of our depth here.'

'I know,' I said wearily. 'And I realise this is more about me than about you.'

I could tell Dad wasn't any happier about leaving than I was. He just didn't want to get me killed.

'We managed to come to some sort of arrangement with the Sicilian Mafia,' he said grumpily. 'But these Triads seem to be far worse. A savage attack the moment we arrive, another a few hours later. I'm still expecting exploding soap in the bathroom, or a missile attack on the hotel suite!'

'Let's hope Mr Wu was right,' I said. 'Instead of our being dead and gone, maybe they'll settle for just gone.'

We chatted for a while longer, but we were both feeling low, and neither of us had much to say.

After a while we said our goodnights. We retired to our respective bathrooms – the suite had two of everything. We both had long hot soaks in enormous bathtubs, and went to bed.

As often happens when you're really tired, I found it hard to get to sleep. I was still worrying about the angry ghost haunting the ruined temple. I couldn't help feeling that I'd let it down. Now the ghost was angry with me as well. It seemed like a very bad idea to get on the wrong side of Jiang Shing, The Executioner – even if he had been dead for hundreds of years!

Mr Wu's words came back to me. 'Ghosts are very real in Hong Kong . . .'

I managed to drift off to sleep at last . . .

I awoke in a cold sweat from a confusing dream of sailing junks and dragons. My heart was pounding and I was terrified.

Then I realised why.

The ghost of Master Jiang Shing was standing at the end of my bed.

Chapter Seven

JOURNEY WITH A GHOST

I was absolutely petrified.

A glowing figure hovering at the end of your bed takes you straight back to childhood.

All those nights when you lay in bed, too old for a nightlight – but still terrified that there's something ghastly lurking under the bed, in the toy cupboard or behind the curtains.

I sat up bolt upright in bed. I can't absolutely swear that my hair stood on end but that's how it felt.

The ghost looked stern and angry, and its eyes glowed a fierce red. It raised its hand and beckoned. The message was clear. It wanted me to go with it.

I didn't want to go. But something else was even clearer.

Somehow the ghost had me in its power.

Gripped by the force of its will, I had no choice. I had to obey.

Reluctantly I got out of bed and scrambled into my clothes. When I was dressed Jiang Shing turned towards the door.

'Listen,' I said. My voice came out as a hoarse croak. 'That door's locked, and my father has the key. And there should be a guard outside the door. Several guards.'

Jiang Shing brushed my warning aside with an impatient gesture. He waved a long, thin hand and the locked door swung slowly open.

There was a security guard outside all right.

He stood rigidly to attention, eyes wide open, staring into space. He didn't seem to see us as we passed by.

The security guard along the corridor and the one by the lift stood in exactly the same pose.

I pressed the button and after a moment the lift appeared. Jiang Shing got in beside me and we rode down to the ground floor.

We came out of the lift and walked across the luxurious hotel lobby. There were a couple of hotel clerks behind the reception desk, a porter, and a group of noisy tourists, just back from some night-spot.

They didn't see us either.

We walked down the hotel steps and into the quiet, tree-lined street.

With the ghost of Jiang Shing at my side, I walked down through the streets of the Peak and on into the bustle of Central.

It was a strange, terrifying experience.

Hong Kong is a late-night town and lots of bars and cafés were still open. The pavements were still crowded, though not quite as busy at midnight as at midday. I could hear the busy sounds of Hong Kong's nightlife, but at a distance, as though from behind some invisible veil.

Jiang Shing stalked through the bustling streets, me at his side. The crowds parted to let him through, as though they sensed his presence without even seeing him.

They didn't seem to see me either.

I felt like a ghost myself. I felt as if I were already dead.

Perhaps I would be soon.

Why else had Jiang Shing summoned me, if not to punish me for letting him down?

In ghastly silence we glided past the skyscrapers of Central and into the more old-fashioned streets beyond, past crowded cafés and late-night food stalls. It was the route we'd taken earlier in the limousine, and the journey seemed to pass almost as quickly.

Hong Kong is crowded but it's not all that big and the distance wasn't great. Jiang Shing glided effortlessly along, and I was somehow carried along beside him.

We came to the harbour and walked on towards the development area. Lights from the vessels in the crowded harbour sparkled on the water. We seemed to reach the site in no time at all.

Jiang Shing strode towards the gate, and the security guards stood to attention, gazing blankly past us like the ones at the hotel. The gate swung open and we moved through it and on to the site. The place was deserted, lit by a scattering of security lights on tall poles.

Jiang Shing led me across the muddy ground and up the little hill towards the ruined temple.

What now? I wondered.

Was I going to be found here in the morning, face down in the mud, the wounds from an invisible ghost dagger in my back?

Jiang Shing raised his hand and pointed.

There was a shaft of light gleaming from the ruins and we moved towards it.

Or rather I did.

I suddenly realised that Jiang Shing's ghost had disappeared. Instead of being relieved, I was even more scared. For a moment I just stood there, shivering on the darkened hillside.

I made an effort to pull myself together. I'd wanted to investigate further. Here was my chance.

The ghost brought me here to see something, I thought. So I'd better see it.

Bracing myself, I moved on towards the light.

Inside the temple, two men were talking in low voices. An old-fashioned lantern stood on a pile of rubble between them.

One of the men was the hatchet-faced Major Chang. The other was Half-Ear Huang, the Triad gangster who had brought the bomb to the restaurant.

They weren't so much talking as arguing furiously. Even though I couldn't understand a word they said, that much was clear.

Major Chang seemed to be accusing, Huang defending himself. Somehow I knew they were talking about the botched bombing attack.

Half-Ear Huang's tone changed from defending himself to one of demand.

At first Major Chang objected. Then, angrily, he gave way. He pulled a huge wad of notes, American dollars, from his pocket and thrust them at Huang, who stowed them away inside his tunic.

Major Chang snapped an angry question. Huang picked up the lantern and led him further into the ruins. Cautiously I moved after them.

Inside the temple Huang kicked aside some rubble to reveal an iron ring set into a flagstone. He bent down, heaved up the flagstone and put it to one side, revealing a square opening underneath. He held the lantern over the opening so that Major Chang could see what was inside.

The dark square was the entrance to some kind of cellar. Inside the cellar were piles of wooden crates.

Huang lowered the lantern into the cellar so that Major Chang could see more clearly.

I moved closer still.

Peering between the two men, I could just make out the letters stencilled on the top of the nearest crate.

There was a Chinese symbol. Below that was a black skull and crossbones. Below that, in English, were the words DANGER – HIGH EXPLOSIVES.

I moved closer to make sure and stumbled over

a little heap of broken tiles. They clattered noisily to the ground and both men swung round.

Major Chang snatched the holstered revolver from his belt.

'I find you in strange company, Major Chang,' I said.

He stared hard at me, his black eyes gleaming with anger. 'You do not seem very surprised,' he said in his slow, heavily accented English.

'I've been wondering why you deliberately shot down a prisoner who might have talked. How the Triad seemed to know exactly when and where to find us. How you came to be called away from lunch so conveniently, just before your friend here delivered his surprise package. Now I know.'

'Now you know,' agreed Major Chang. 'Unfortunately for you, you know too much.' He turned to Huang. 'Kill him – silently. We will deal with the father later – after the explosion.'

Huang seemed to hesitate for a moment. Then he produced a large knife from under his tunic. He tossed it up and caught it by the blade, ready to throw.

'Kill him!' snarled Major Chang.

He moved some distance away to give Huang a clear throw.

I tensed myself, ready to turn and run.

Not that there was any point in it.

I knew I'd end up with the knife between my shoulder blades. Even if Huang missed, which didn't seem likely, there was still Major Chang and his revolver.

I was going to die with a dagger in my back after all. Not a ghost dagger, but the very real knife of a Triad killer.

This was my punishment for disappointing Master Jiang Shing.

The ghost had brought me here to be killed.

It was a living nightmare, and I had no chance of escape. Or like a play – a play whose end had already been written.

Huang raised his arm; I was poised to turn and run . . .

Suddenly the ghost of Jiang Shing stood there before us. Huang froze into a statue – and so did Major Chang.

The face of the ghost was blazing with fury, and its eyes glowed red. It raised a hand and pointed accusingly, first at Huang and then at Major Chang. Slowly, unwillingly, Huang turned to face Major Chang.

For a moment we all stood motionless.

Jiang Shing's bony hand swept out in a commanding gesture. Huang's arm flashed down – and the knife thudded into the heart of Major Chang.

Major Chang stared down at the knife-hilt in astonishment.

He clutched at it and crumpled to the ground.

Huang stood like a statue, still poised from his throw. He stared down at Major Chang's body, as if unable to realise what he had done.

Jiang Shing pointed an accusing finger at Huang, his face stern. Huang gasped and dropped to his knees, head bowed.

I looked at Jiang Shing. 'All right,' I said shakily. 'Are we done?'

The ghost of Master Jiang Shing nodded solemnly – and slowly faded away.

I walked over to the kneeling Huang and stood looking down at him. Somehow I knew exactly what I had to say.

'Do you hear me, Huang?'

'I hear you, master.' His voice was a terrified whisper.

'Your deal with Major Chang is at an end. As you see, this project is under the protection of Master Jiang Shing. All who try to harm it will suffer his curse. Do you understand?'

'I understand, master. It shall be as you command. I shall inform the Triads.'

'All right. Get up.'

Huang got slowly to his feet. He bowed low before me. 'Forgive me, master. I did not know you were one of the Enlightened, or I would not have dared to attempt to harm you.'

'No more bombs or bullets?'

He bowed again. 'From now on you and your honoured father will be under the protection of the Triad.' He hesitated. 'I have offended greatly. What is to be my fate?'

Suddenly I felt very tired. 'You'd better go,' I said wearily. 'This place will be swarming with security guards soon.'

Huang stared at me as if he couldn't believe his luck. He disappeared into the darkness.

I turned and plodded over to the site hut.

I hammered on the door until Douggie Henderson appeared in a lurid pair of red and white-striped pyjamas. He blinked down at me in amazement. 'Strewth, it's young Matt Stirling. How did you get here?'

'It's a long story,' I said. 'Get some clothes on and come over to the ruined temple. I've got something to show you.'

'Yeah? Like what?'

'Like a dead body and a stack of explosives.'

'Cripes,' said Douggie and disappeared into the hut. He reappeared seconds later in a pair of wellington boots, with a coat over his pyjamas. He was clutching a big torch.

I took him over to the temple and showed him Major Chang's body and the explosives in the hidden cellar.

He shone his torch through the square opening.

'That's the shipment we lost! What the heck's been going on here, Matt?'

'Chang was bribing the Triad to sabotage the project,' I said. 'Don't ask me why. Anyway, there was a quarrel and Chang got killed. The deal's off, so there shouldn't be any more sabotage or delays. The project can go ahead now – on one condition.'

'Just name it!'

'This temple,' I said. 'Don't blow it up or bulldoze it, or you'll be in trouble all over again. It's got to be restored, so it's just as it was over a hundred years ago. Do that and your troubles are probably over. Have you got a phone?'

'Got me mobile back at the hut.'

'Have you got Mr Wu's number?'

'Sure. He gave me his emergency number when the trouble started.'

'Call Mr Wu and tell him to bring Captain Lee and a squad of security guards. They'll sort everything out. Ask Mr Wu to contact my father and tell him I'm safe and well and everything's all right. Oh, and one more thing?'

'What's that?'

'I could murder a cup of tea!'

I was drinking a cup of tea with Douggie in the doorway of the site office when a convoy of three cars roared on to the site. Mr Wu, Captain Lee and my father jumped out of the first, and a squad of security guards piled out of the other two.

Douggie collared Mr Wu and Captain Lee and took them over to the temple.

I went back into the hut with my tea. Dad followed me, steaming with rage. I'd never seen him so angry. As he drew breath to yell at me I said, 'Did you get my message? It's over. I'm safe and well, everything's all right.'

'Everything is far from all right, young man! I don't know what's been happening yet, but how dare you take the appalling risk of coming over here alone?'

'I wasn't alone,' I said. 'I had company. Sit down and have a cup of tea and I'll tell you about it.'

I poured him a cup of tea and told him the whole story. The dream on the plane, the warning visions at the airport and the restaurant, the ghost in my room. I told him of our strange journey, of events at the site, and the death of Major Chang.

When I finished he was a lot calmer, but still very sceptical.

'You really expect me to believe all this, Matthew?'

'That's up to you,' I said. 'You were there at the airport, and at the restaurant. Something saved both our lives. There's a dead body and a pile of stolen explosives at the temple – they're both real enough.'

Dad shook his head. 'Yes, but even so . . . an avenging Chinese ghost!'

I told you he's sceptical about the supernatural.

'Can you suggest some other explanation for what happened tonight?' I asked.

Dad was struggling desperately for a rational, nonsupernatural answer. 'Perhaps you were dreaming, Matthew,' he said at last. 'Maybe you sleepwalked here. You used to sleepwalk, didn't you? And with all this on your mind . . .'

'And Chang's dead body and the explosives?'

Dad shrugged. 'You turned up here unexpectedly and stumbled upon the meeting. Perhaps the conspirators quarrelled – and this man Huang killed Major Chang.'

'Perhaps,' I said. 'But consider this. Our hotel room and this site were both locked and under armed guard.'

Dad frowned. 'So?'

'So how did I get out of one and into the other without anyone seeing me?'

Dad was silent for a moment. He leaned forward and put a hand on my shoulder. 'Well, as long as you're really all right . . .'

'You believe me, then?'

'I believe *you* believe all you've told me,' said Dad. 'For myself, I don't know if you were dreaming, or in a trance or hypnotised, or . . .'

'Remember what Mr Wu said, Dad, when we first arrived.'

'What?'

'In Hong Kong, ghosts are very real.'

We were enjoying a late breakfast in our suite when Mr Wu arrived. He'd been up all night but he was still fizzing with excitement.

'You know what those scoundrels were planning to do?' he told us. 'They were going to blow up part of the harbour wall, and flood the project and much of the area around. It would have been a catastrophe!'

'I still don't really understand *why*,' said Dad. 'What were Major Chang's motives?'

'They were – political,' said Mr Wu. 'Even in China, we have politics. I must ask for your discretion.'

'Of course,' said Dad. 'We must give Ms Alexander a report, but nobody else will hear a word.'

'That goes for me too,' I said.

Mr Wu paused for a moment, clearly embarrassed. 'There are those in my government who wish, as I do myself, for Hong Kong to be our bridge to the West,' he said. 'Others wish to isolate Hong Kong and China from the world. Major Chang belonged to the latter faction. The harbour project was the first major collaboration with the West since Hong Kong reverted to China . . .'

'So if it failed disastrously . . .' I said.

'Precisely,' said Mr Wu. 'Many people in China would start to believe that no good could come of collaboration with the West.'

Dad said, 'And Western businessmen would

say it was impossible to get anything done in Hong Kong since China took over.'

'All of which is what Chang and his faction wanted,' said Mr Wu. 'They used their political influence to hinder the harbour project with bureaucratic delays. Then Major Chang misused his secret intelligence funds to bribe the Triad into sabotage.'

'How do you know all this?' I asked.

'Major Chang was a very well-organised man,' said Mr Wu happily. 'Fortunately he kept detailed records of his evil schemes in a notebook. I found it on his body! With this knowledge I can put an end to the bureaucratic delays. All in all, I owe you – my country owes you – a great debt.'

'Matthew is the one you should thank,' said Dad generously. 'All I did was complain and demand to go home!'

'Let us turn to happier matters, Professor Stirling,' said Mr Wu tactfully. 'Now the danger from the Triad is over you must enjoy your stay in Hong Kong. I have taken the liberty of cancelling today's departure, and I have reinstated your cancelled lecture at the space museum. There are several very fine restaurants we have yet to visit . . .'

*　*　*

That was about it, really.

We spent several more days in Hong Kong, saw most of the sights and visited many more restaurants with Mr Wu. I still didn't manage to tackle the chicken feet, though.

Dad delivered his lecture at the space museum to great applause.

We went back to the site to say goodbye to Douggie and found him hard at work and happy.

Official permits were arriving by every post, and lorry-loads of materials were turning up by the minute.

All the workmen were back and hard at work.

Thanks to the protection of the Triad, nobody dared steal so much as a rusty nail.

We promised to come back for the grand opening when the project was complete.

'Don't forget the temple,' I said as we left.

'No worries,' said Douggie. 'We've set up a committee to look after the restoration. Your mate Chalmers is in charge.'

Later we went to say goodbye to Chalmers and found him happily studying old plans and making lists of Chinese craftsmen . . .

'I think Master Jiang Shing will be pleased with the final result,' said Chalmers.

'He'd better be,' I warned. 'Believe me, he's not someone you want getting mad at you!'

A few days later we said goodbye to Mr Chalmers, Mr Wu and Captain Lee at the airport, and went to board our plane.

There was still one more goodbye to be said.

I was hanging about in the VIP lounge, waiting for Dad to come back from complaining about ten minutes' delay in our departure time.

Suddenly I felt a presence close beside me and the now all-too-familiar chilling of the blood.

I turned and saw a fierce-looking old Chinese gentleman. He was very tall and thin and he wore a traditional, high-collared robe. He wasn't floating or glowing or doing anything weird. Just standing there, his face stern and impassive.

But I recognised him all the same. We'd once been for a long walk together.

He looked at me steadily for a moment.

Then he bowed. Beneath the long moustaches, his thin lips moved in what might even have been a smile.

I bowed in return. 'Goodbye, Master Jiang Shing.'

He bowed again and moved away.

I was still staring after him when Dad came bustling up.

'We'll be leaving in just a few minutes,' he announced. 'Who was that old-fashioned-looking character you were talking to?'

'Just an old Chinese gentleman,' I said.

'What did he want?'

'I'm not really sure,' I said. 'I rather think he was thanking me for what we'd done here.'

I turned to look after the old man but he had disappeared.

'Well, that was very kind of him,' said Dad. 'Odd type to find in the VIP lounge, though.'

'Don't you believe it, Dad,' I said. 'That was a Very Important Person indeed!'

They called our flight, and we headed for the departure gate.